THE PEPPER PARTY

Family Feud Face-Off

THE PEPPER PARTY IS JUST GETTING STARTED!

THE PEPPER PARTY

Family Feud Face-Off

BY

JAY COOPER

Scholastic Inc.

For Dad, who (thankfully) never
forced air horn lessons on me

Copyright © 2019 by Jay Cooper

All rights reserved. Published by Scholastic Inc., *Publishers since 1920*. SCHOLASTIC and associated logos are trademarks and/or registered trademarks of Scholastic Inc.

The publisher does not have any control over and does not assume any responsibility for author or third-party websites or their content.

No part of this publication may be reproduced, stored in a retrieval system, or transmitted in any form or by any means, electronic, mechanical, photo-copying, recording, or otherwise, without written permission of the publisher. For information regarding permission, write to Scholastic Inc., Attention: Permissions Department, 557 Broadway, New York, NY 10012.

This book is a work of fiction. Names, characters, places, and incidents are either the product of the author's imagination or are used fictitiously, and any resemblance to actual persons, living or dead, business establishments, events, or locales is entirely coincidental.

ISBN 978-1-338-29704-1

10 9 8 7 6 5 4 3 2 1   19 20 21 22 23
Printed in the U.S.A.   40
First printing, June 2019
Book design by Nina Goffi and Christopher Stengel

Maria Pepper always made her bed the moment she got up.

Her favorite book was titled *How to Make Friends, Influence People, and Crush Your Enemies into Dust.* This is what it says about beds: *You think Genghis Khan didn't make his*

bed before he rode off and pillaged a village? HA!
A messy bed means a messy life.

Maria definitely did *not* have a messy life. She kept her room clean, orderly, and organized. In other words, everything was perfectly perfect.

Well . . . nearly everything. Only half the room was hers. The other side, which belonged to her sister Annie, was always a total disaster. Half-read comic books, half-completed art projects, half a hoagie, and half a hundred other long-discarded things lay everywhere.

Maria never did anything halfway.

She'd been that way ever since she was a baby. Infant Maria had learned to change her own diapers. She'd skipped first words and gone straight to complete sentences. Apparently, perfection was in the Pepper genes. Sadly, she got all of it, leaving none for her brothers and sisters.

On her way to the bathroom, Maria stepped over Annie's Chihuahua, Azzie, and into something squishy. It turned out to be a half-eaten slice of pizza her sister had left on the floor. She looked down at a bit of pepperoni poking up between her toes.

She hopped out of the room on one leg, the slice of pizza dragging behind her by a long string of cheese stuck to her foot.

Maria wanted to scream, but she had bigger fish to fry. It was the first day of the mascot contest at San Pimento Grade School.

Maria smiled. It was a contest she planned to win.

But when she entered the kitchen, her smile vanished. The room was full of her brothers and sisters eating breakfast before school, and they were already being incredibly, annoyingly Peppery.

Maria tried to ignore everyone. It wasn't easy.

Her big sister, Megs, was spinning what looked like a cross between a basketball and a pancake on her finger. She lost control and the wobbly-looking ball knocked over a glass of orange juice onto Maria's plate.

"Megs!" Maria cried.

"Sorry! I'm just trying to get my froosbet-ball working before school!"

Maria didn't know what a "froosbetball" was, and she didn't care. She sighed and turned to get some cereal, but her brother Ricky was blocking the way.

He was practicing a crazy hip-hop dance move where his arms waved every which way in fast, jerky motions. Every time Maria made for the cereal box she had to pull back quickly or he'd wallop her.

"Ricky! Stop it! I can't get to the Wheaty Oats!"

But Ricky couldn't hear her. He had his headphones on and was singing along to a rap song.

5

1. Maria Pepper (age 9) Plotting to win school mascot contest
2. Megs Pepper (age 10) Creating a new sport
3. Scoochy (age 2) Being a mess, as usual
4. Tee Pepper (Mom) Running late for work

5. Ricky Pepper (age 12) Practicing his dance moves
6. Annie Pepper (age 8) Reporting SPN News
7. Beta Max Pepper (age 9) Filming SPN News
8. Sal Pepper (Dad) Cooking chili
9. Meemaw Pepper (ancient) Looking for her teeth

She tried yelling, "RICKY! LET ME HAVE SOME WHEATY OATS!!!"

Meemaw, who had lost her dentures, snapped her fingers. "The Wheaty Oats! That's where I left 'em!" She easily ducked Ricky's elbow and grabbed the cereal box. Meemaw dug around in the box and pulled out her lost set of teeth. She popped them into her mouth and gave her granddaughter a big, false-toothed grin.

Maria suddenly lost her appetite.

Their father, Sal, spoke up from where he was cooking his nearly-award-winning chili. "Hey, kiddos! Are you all excited to see your dear old dad at school today? It's my very first day as lunch lady! I'm mixing up a nice, tasty batch of chili to celebrate!"

Their mother, Tee, kissed him on the cheek. "I think the term is *lunch person*, dear."

Scoochy threw scrambled eggs in Maria's hair. "MARIA GOTS SCRAMBLED HAIR!" the two-year-old cackled.

There were days when Maria couldn't stand her family. And then there were days when she *really* couldn't stand them.

Pulling egg out of her hair, she decided to leave for school. She wanted to be there before anyone else, anyway. But a microphone was shoved rudely in her face the minute she opened the front door. Annie held the microphone, while her brother Beta blinded Maria with the light from his video camera.

"Annie Pepper, San Pimento Network News! May I ask you a few questions about the Pimento Olive mascot contest, Miss Pepper? What's your stand on cartwheels? Are you hiding a pimento allergy? The public has a right to know!"

Maria pushed away Beta's camera. "No interviews!"

Annie whined, "Aw, c'mon, sis! The San Pimento mascot competition is a big story! It's just the thing we need for our next segment!"

Becoming a volunteer reporter for the local television station had been Annie's idea. Beta had agreed to be her cameraperson. So far they'd done one story about Frida Flamingo's Animal Adoption Agency. Frida, a big movie star, had given them an exclusive interview, and the people down at the local television station had loved it! They thought the story had everything: a celebrity, human interest, and most important, lots of cute animals!

Now Annie and Beta needed their next scoop. Annie thought that a story on the school mascot competition might be just the thing.

Maria had her doubts about letting her brother and sister interview her. She was worried they would make her look silly on television in classic Pepper fashion. "Sorry, guys," she said as she started to push past them.

But somehow Annie's microphone cable wrapped around her legs. Maria tripped over the cable and went tumbling down the front steps, landing on her butt in the flower bed. She gave Annie a dirty look.

Annie grimaced. "Sorry, sis!" Then she whispered to Beta: "You got that? Tell me you got that!"

Beta nodded and winked.

Maria was not amused. This wasn't the first

time her family had embarrassed her. The list was already really long.

There was the time Megs's football team had crushed her science fair volcano project in a pile-on tackle in the living room. Her cheeks reddened when she thought of how Beta had kept stealing her favorite lunch (spaghetti and tomato sauce) to use as vampire makeup for one of his horror movies. Then there was the incident when Ricky had sobbed wildly after his girlfriend broke up with him during Maria's solo in the school musical. And who could forget the time Annie had accidentally washed her red superhero cape with Maria's white chorus shirt? (Making her the only pink singer in a sea of white.)

But none of these could compete with her father insisting on dropping her off at all of her debates in his food truck, the Chili Chikka-Wow-Wow, his mustache dripping with tastes of his latest chili flavor. And EVERYBODY always saw it.

It was a miracle she hadn't disowned them by now. And this mascot contest was way too important to let the Peppers mess it up.

CHAPTER 2

Just inside the main doors of the San Pimento Grade School, Maria set up a table. She hung a sign that read:

CHOOSE MARIA PEPPER!
SAN PIMENTO'S
PERFECT SCHOOL MASCOT!

To Maria, the chance to wear the Olive mascot costume was the highest honor at San Pimento Grade School. The Olive appeared at all the school sporting events, and it even rode on a float in the homecoming parade! Past Pimento Olives had gone on to become senators, heads of corporations—one had even become a famous talk show host!

Anyone who signed up could campaign for school mascot for one week. On Friday there would be tryouts onstage in front of the entire school. Afterward students would vote to crown the next San Pimento Olive. The crown in this case was a giant toothpick that poked through the costume's head.

Once she hung the sign, Maria made sure her campaign buttons were rotated the exact same way and her flyers were perfectly stacked. Proud of her work, she waited for the students to arrive.

She waited.

And waited.

But nobody came through the front door.

Where was everyone???

Then she heard music trickling through the front doors of the school. It sounded like . . . was that . . . an *ice cream truck jingle*?

Curious, she followed the tinny sounds.

As soon as she opened the door, Maria saw where all the students were.

Everyone was crowding around an ice cream truck parked in front of the school. They all jostled and pushed their way to the window, like a bunch of zombies hungry for brains. And serving them all was someone's wrinkly old *butler*! An old man in a tuxedo leaned through the window and handed out free ice cream sundaes to the students. With a slightly shaky bow, he offered one to Maria.

Next to the butler stood a boy wearing a very snazzy suit. She knew she hadn't laid eyes on him before—you'd remember a kid in a suit like that.

The boy handed Maria a T-shirt with his smiling face printed on it. "I know what you're thinking," he said. "'Ice cream sundaes first thing on a Monday? That Darren Dill must be crazy!' Just crazy enough to become this school's next mascot!"

Maria was speechless . . . something that had never happened to her before.

Annie and Beta had pushed their way

ICE CREAM

through the crowd to join her. "This Darren Dill kid's amazing! Beta, we HAVE to interview him," said Annie.

The butler handed them each an ice cream sundae. Beta said, "Maybe after we chow down." He stuffed a spoonful of ice cream in his mouth.

Maria squinted her eyes furiously. It seemed she had some competition.

How to Make Friends, Influence People, and Crush Your Enemies into Dust had a chapter on war. *To conquer your enemy, learn everything about them. Know their every fear, their every wish, their every booger!* So at lunch, Maria asked her two best friends, Lavonia and Roger, about the new kid as they moved along the cafeteria line.

"His full name is actually Darren Dill *the Fourth*. He literally has an *I* and a *V* at the end of his name. That means he must be pretty fancy!" said Lavonia.

"Fancy and SUPERrich," claimed Roger. "I saw him show up for school in a stretch limousine! And I hear he lives in some ritzy penthouse uptown . . ."

"Well, I heard he's an orphan," said Lavonia. "He lives alone with his butler. No one knows what happened to his family . . ."

Maria had a guilty thought. As sad as being an orphan must be, life without her crazy parents and her dumb brothers and sisters sounded kind of awesome.

She felt kind of bad for Darren. But not bad enough to let him become the next San Pimento Olive!

"I can't believe he's trying to *buy* everyone's votes with frozen treats!" Maria said.

"That'll (chew) never (chew) work (chew) . . ." Roger said through a mouthful of ice cream sandwich.

"I don't know." Lavonia shrugged. "This is top-quality dairy."

Maria scowled.

Then a loud voice called out, "Hey, pumpkin! Want some mmm-mmm-good chili?"

Her father was standing behind the lunch counter.

He beamed at her and her friends with a big, oafish grin.

Maria screamed, "YAAAAAAH!!!"

A panicked Sal dove under the counter.

Maria had forgotten that today was her father's first day working in the cafeteria.

Roger snickered. "Your *dad* is the new lunch lady?"

"Lunch *person*." Sal stood. "Chili? Courtesy of the Chili Chikka-Wow-Wow!"

He slopped chili onto their trays and then, in a booming voice he usually used only at county fairs and football games, declared,

"Don't forget: Maria Pepper for San Pimento Olive! She's the best Pepper for the job!"

The entire lunchroom stopped eating and stared.

If she could have, Maria would have died of embarrassment.

At dinner Tuesday evening, Annie and Beta announced that they had a big surprise for the family—a brand-new segment of theirs would air on the local news that very night!

Everyone was excited to see it. Their mom even popped popcorn for the event.

When Annie appeared on-screen, the family cheered!

"Hello, I'm Annie Pepper with SPN News. Tonight, we take you inside the posh lifestyle of San Pimento Grade School's newest student,  Darren Dill IV. Join me as we get a glimpse into the life of the richest, most powerful fourth grader in town."

Maria couldn't believe it. Darren Dill had actually let Annie and Beta interview him. She smiled to herself. They were sure to make a fool out of him!

Annie titled the segment *Superpads of the Crazy Rich and Almost Definitely Future School*

Mascots. (That last part was payback for her sister refusing her interview.) In the segment, Annie and Beta rode up a glass elevator to the penthouse Darren lived in with his butler. There, Darren gave them a personal tour of his spectacular space!

Maria's head began to spin as she watched her own sister *ooh* and *ahh* all over Darren's amazing stuff. Darren's apartment was huge! It was full of fancy artwork and white leather furniture. And there were no messes anywhere, no muddy sneakers, no half-drunk glasses of chocolate milk. Everything in Darren's apartment was in its place, gleaming and spotless.

At one point during the tour, Annie spied a door marked TOP SECRET. She tried to take a peek inside, but Darren's butler, Crinklebottom, blocked her. Instead, Darren led her to a room

across the hall that was full of nothing but sneakers from floor to ceiling!

From behind the camera, Maria heard Beta gasp, "Holy shlamoly!"

During the interview, Darren admitted that he was excited about moving to San Pimento, and even more excited about the idea of being elected the San Pimento Olive.

"What do your parents say about your mascoting dreams?"

Darren looked stiff for a moment, and then he smiled. "Well, I'm an orphan, Annie. But if my parents were around, they'd be very excited about it." His smile widened. "In fact, I'm certain they would be shocked."

Maria couldn't believe it. Annie and Beta had not made Darren look dumb at all. They had made him look great. The interview would help his chances of becoming the Olive!

"Why would you interview Darren Dill when you know I'm competing against him for school mascot?" she yelled.

Annie's jaw dropped. "Are you kidding me??? I asked you for an interview first, and you turned me down. You can't be mad at me for interviewing someone else if you said no."

Annie crossed her arms, daring Maria to say something back.

But Maria just growled, stomped off to their bedroom, and slammed the door.

She paced back and forth across the half-messy, half-clean room and considered her next move. She needed to get the spotlight back on her. Maybe a catchy musical jingle might do the trick . . .

She dug her dusty old electronic keyboard

from the back of her closet and began to play with an idea. Her audience (all the Pepper pets) seemed to approve, as long as you ignored how Elvis the lovebird covered his ears with his wings.

Just as she was putting the finishing touches on her song, Ricky appeared in the doorway.

"That's pretty great, sis. I bet it would make an amazing rap song."

Ricky's last girlfriend had dumped him because she had fallen head over heels for a hip-hop star. Jordan Jamz had these REALLY popular videos on Y'allTube where he won rap and break-dancing competitions. Now Ricky

was determined to become the best freestyler in all of San Pimento.

Maria didn't want to hurt Ricky's feelings, but she thought writing a rap was a terrible idea.

"Thanks, Ricky, but I think I've got this," Maria said.

He shrugged and walked off to brush his teeth for bed.

CHAPTER 4

At school the next morning the principal, Ms. Macaroon, let Maria read the announcements over the intercom. Afterward, Maria sang her jingle for the entire school:

"Everyone across the school,
They're voting for Maria.

Other mascots aren't as cool,
We're voting for Maria!
Vote for Maria, TODAY!"

She ended by saying, "This message was approved by the Choose Maria for San Pimento Olive Mascot Coalition."

By lunchtime, Maria was feeling great. A lot of people had told her that they'd loved her song. Or at least, Roger and Lavonia had. Two was a lot, right?

But Maria's good mood came to a screeching standstill when she stopped at her locker to drop off her math book between math and pick up her English homework.

She was surprised to see a slip of paper stuck in the door.

She pulled it out and read it:

Maria,

Since you're so musically talented, I offer you a challenge. Meet me after school at the football bleachers for a rap battle. You against me. We're each allowed one backup rapper.

Darren Dill IV

P.S. I've put invitations in everyone's lockers, so if you still want to become the San Pimento Olive, I wouldn't back down.

Maria looked around. Up and down the hallway, kids were pulling flyers from their lockers and looking at her excitedly.

A rap battle??? B-b-but, but I can't rap! She panicked.

Luckily, she knew someone who could. Even now, he was racing around the corner, holding one of Darren's flyers in his hand.

35

Ricky was beaming. "It's on, sis! Darren Dill has no idea who he's messing with!"

"Oh brother," she mumbled.

He wrapped an arm tightly around her neck. "I know. Aren't you glad that yours is so awesome?"

At the end of the day, Maria and Ricky walked out to the football field. The stands were packed with students. Half the school was there! Maria spied her family in the crowd. Megs waved happily. Beta gave her a thumbs-up.

Annie frowned at her. She and Maria weren't speaking.

Two microphones were set up in front of the stands, but Darren was nowhere in sight.

"Don't worry," said Ricky. "We got this. I've been practicing really hard. There's no way Darren Dill can out-rap me!"

Maria wished she was as confident.

The crowd waited expectantly.

"Huh," said Ricky. "Maybe Darren chickened out when he heard he'd be up against MC Ricky P!"

Maria rolled her eyes.

Suddenly a deafening beat started thumping over the football field's loudspeakers.

Maria, Ricky, and the entire student body turned around. Up in the announcer's booth, Darren's butler, Crinklebottom, had set up a bunch of deejay equipment. He started spinning records in time to the thumping beat. His shakiness made him a natural record scratcher.

Darren came out from behind the stands, dressed as always in a snazzy suit. He grabbed a microphone. "San Pimento, are you ready for a rap battle?"

The crowd went wild.

He turned to Maria and Ricky. "You've brought your second, I see."

Ricky winked at Maria and grabbed his own microphone.

"Yeah, I'm her number two,
I'm here to rap for you,
but your butler better bring it
when you tell him to!"

Ricky finished with a couple of slick break-dancing moves.

The crowd clapped and whooped. Maria was impressed. Ricky was pretty good!

Darren laughed. "Oh, Crinklebottom isn't my second. He's a great deejay, but a lousy rapper. No, my second should be showing up right about . . . now."

A bright red SUV with spinning hubcaps drove through a gate at the opposite end of the field. The license plate spelled JAMZ. Which spelled disaster for Maria.

The rap battle was a massacre.

Jordan Jamz exited the SUV as the crowd roared. He seemed to have as many people with him as he had gold chains, and Jordan Jamz had A LOT of gold chains. But he wasn't just flash. Jamz was really good. So good that Ricky

Lady Bling

Steve

MC Jerz-E

Illumin-Natey

Jordan Jamz!

Lil' Mink

Fresh Lord Arkon

could only stand there with his mouth hanging open. Over the next half hour, Jordan destroyed poor Ricky in the rap battle.

At one point, Jordan Jamz had everyone in the stands rapping along with him. They all cried, "Who's wiggity wack? Maria Pepper! Who's wackity wig? Maria Pepper!"

Maria shook her brother hard. "Ricky! Snap out of it! You have to help me! We're losing!"

But Ricky was like a zombie. His mind was

a blank. He just stuttered, "Duh . . . uh . . . uh . . . uh . . ."

By now, Jordan had the whole crowd chanting along with him:

Maria threw up her hands at Darren. "Jordan Jamz? You hired *Jordan Jamz* to rap for you?"

Darren looked at Maria and shrugged. "You know the old saying: *If someone challenges you to a kazoo fight, bring the whole orchestra . . .*"

Maria finished the quote. "*But leave the triangle at home. That's just mean.*" Of course she knew that saying. It was from *How to Make Friends, Influence People, and Crush Your Enemies into Dust.* Clearly Darren had read it, too.

CHAPTER 5

The next day, all anyone was talking about was Jordan Jamz and the rap battle. The gossip followed Maria all the way to lunch, where Sal was serving chili *again*. Today the sign in front of his station read: SAL'S SERIOUSLY SPICY SRIRACHA CHILI. As he ladled the goop into bowls, he said things like "Maria's your man!

Er, *wo*-man, that is!" and "Maria Pepper's the perfect Pimento!"

She let him fill up her own tray and then slumped into her seat next to Lavonia and Roger, who were careful not to bring up Darren Dill.

Instead Roger started telling jokes, hoping to cheer Maria up a little. Between spoonfuls of chili, Roger had Maria and Lavonia giggling at his gutbusters. He was halfway through his chili and getting to the punch line of a really funny one when the *Incident* happened.

"So the dentist sticks his head into the lion's mouth and says, 'Let me know when it hurts.' And the lion says . . ."

The girls started laughing. But Roger wasn't.

"That wasn't the punch line. That was my stomach."

Not half a second later, Lavonia's stomach rumbled, too. Even louder.

Then a loud roar echoed throughout the cafeteria. It was the sound of hundreds of stomachs filled with Sal's Seriously Spicy Sriracha Chili complaining at the exact same time.

GRRRRrrrrRRRRRooOOOwwLLL!

"Uh-oh," said Sal. "Maybe I put a bit *too* much spice in the chili . . ."

Roger suddenly stood up, holding his stomach, and sprinted for the bathroom as fast as his legs would take him.

But the cranky lunchroom monitor, Ms. Meany, was blocking his path.

"Where're you runnin' to, mister? Hmm?"

"Sorry, Ms. Meany, but I gotta go! I GOTTA GO NOW!!!" He pushed his way past the cafeteria monitor.

"Well, I never!" Ms. Meany exclaimed, watching him dash down the hall.

She turned back around just in time to see a mob of students stampeding straight for her. They trampled her in their rush to the bathroom.

Maria watched the entire cafeteria empty out.

Finally, only Ms. Meany remained, sprawled out on the floor and groaning about a bruised spleen. Maria looked over at her dad. He stuck a finger in his chili and tasted it. "Nope, that's the usual amount of spice!"

Great, Maria thought. *Who's going to vote for*

the girl whose dad gave the whole school the runs???
She left the cafeteria, fighting back tears.
Everything was going so terribly! Darren was
winning, and her own family was helping him.

Even worse, tomorrow were the tryouts in
front of the entire school!

Maria pictured Darren Dill being crowned
San Pimento Olive. She saw him waving at the
crowds in that sacred, puffy costume as his
limousine led the homecoming parade.

In a dazc, she shuffled down the
hallway. Just as she walked past
the gym, the door opened,
and a cross between a
pancake and a basket-
ball came flying
through it.

Maria watched it bounce off the wall and wobble across the floor.

Wait a minute, she thought. *I know that ball.* It was the weird flattened basketball that Megs had been fiddling with at breakfast all week.

She picked it up, peeked through the door, and saw Megs and her friends inside.

"Hey, Maria!" Megs smiled. "Check out the cool sport I invented! Will you toss me the froosbetball?"

She bounced the strange ball to her sister, and the gym full of girls immediately took off after it, laughing.

Maria took a seat on the stands, and watched them play what looked like a weird combination of basketball and Frisbee. *What an odd sport*, she thought. But as she watched Megs and her friends dribble the ball and then fling

it at the hoop like a Frisbee, she also thought it looked kind of fun. For a moment she pictured herself as the San Pimento Olive on the sidelines, cheering them on.

Yeah, like that's ever going to happen now, Maria thought.

Megs looked at her sister sitting sadly in the stands. She felt terrible for her. Darren was winning, and everyone knew it.

If only there was some way I could help Maria out!

A friend tossed Megs the froosbetball. An idea popped into her head just as she caught it. It was crazy, but maybe a crazy idea was exactly what Maria needed to win.

6

Maria woke up Friday morning with her stomach tied in knots.

She barely listened in class and spent all morning thinking about a quote from *How to Make Friends, Influence People, and Crush Your Enemies into Dust*:

There is no dishonor in defeat. There may be smelliness in de feet, but there is no dishonor.

Still, Maria hadn't given up hope. She felt she still had a chance if she really wowed them during the talent competition.

In the auditorium, Annie and Beta had set up their camera to air the competition live on SPN News.

"This is Annie Pepper reporting live at the Pimento Olive mascot tryouts. Our candidates are about to take the stage. Will hometown girl Maria Pepper roll to victory? Will megarich Darren Dill make everyone green with envy? Or will one of those other kids do anything to make *olive* us take notice?"

The contenders stood backstage while the rest of the students took their seats, class by

class. Then the show began. One kid did a lousy act with a dummy—everyone could see his lips move. Another twirled a flaming baton, which swung so close to her costume, Ms. Macaroon had to roll her out on the stage floor.

Backstage, Maria quietly ignored Darren.

Suddenly, he turned to her. "Maria, I'd like

us to be friends. I don't have many. None, in fact. Crinklebottom doesn't count."

Maria's jaw dropped. "You're kidding, right? You're my archnemesis!"

Darren laughed. "Of course I am! But only because we're so much alike! I've seen your family. They're ridiculous. I had the same problem with my family. And I have a piece of advice for you: Sometimes you need to give up the things that hold you back."

Maria raised an eyebrow.

The last student's tryout ended with unenthusiastic applause. He walked backstage and threw his baton to the ground in frustration.

Now it was Darren's turn.

He walked out onstage, but he didn't dance or burst into song or anything. Instead, he spoke into the microphone.

"Good afternoon, San Pimento Grade School. The fact is, I really don't care about winning this contest."

The audience laughed.

"No, really. I don't. The main reason I entered was to meet people at a new school that was all the way across the country from where I grew up. It's hard to be new. Being megarich doesn't make me super confident. Sometimes I go overboard, with sundaes and rap battles. But if you vote for me, I promise to be the best San Pimento Olive I can be. Either way, it's been really nice getting to meet all of you this week. Thank you."

Then he pulled out a violin from behind his back and began to play.

The music didn't have the pizzazz that you might expect from a mascot tryout, but it was

beautiful. The haunting melody drifted across the auditorium. It was the prettiest violin playing many of the students had ever heard. A couple of them actually cried.

When he finished, he bowed and left the stage.

The auditorium was silent for a moment, and then suddenly the audience broke out into mad applause.

Maria was flabbergasted. She hadn't expected the kid who had been crushing her all week to be so . . . sweet! And talented!

Ms. Macaroon returned to the microphone, dabbing at her eyes with a tissue.

"Darren, that was beautiful." She blew her nose loudly. "And now our final contestant, Maria Pepper!"

Maria walked up to the microphone, still in shock over Darren's performance.

She took a deep breath and crossed her fingers. *Here we go*, she thought.

But before she could say a thing, bright spotlights and curling fog suddenly swooped across the stage.

CHAPTER 7

Megs's voice boomed over the loudspeakers. "LADIES AND GENTLEMEN, YOUR NEXT SAN PIMENTO OLIVE, MARIA PEPPER, BRINGS YOU SOMETHING COMPLETELY NEW AND TOTALLY DIFFERENT. MARIA BRINGS YOU . . . *FROOSBETBALL!*"

Megs and five of her sporty friends ran onto the stage dribbling froosbetballs. They had matching shirts (unfortunately, they matched with an awkward photo of Maria). Megs wore a fancy headset microphone.

"What kind of a mascot will Maria be?" Megs called out to the crowd. "Inspiring! Visionary! Just like . . . FROOSBETBALL!"

By now the girls had stopped dribbling the froosbetballs and were flinging them to one another like Frisbees.

Maria hissed at her sister, "Megs! What are you doing?"

Megs winked. "Helping you win, sis! What had you planned for the talent competition, anyway?"

Maria had planned to hypnotize someone in the crowd—probably Lavonia, who would have

pretended to be under Maria's spell even if she wasn't really. Thinking about it now, it seemed a bit lame. However, Maria didn't like this hostile takeover of her tryout!

Suddenly a deep, thudding hip-hop beat started playing. Ricky Pepper came onstage in a tracksuit, carrying a giant boom box.

"Yo yo yo! San Pimento! How ya doing!"

Maria whispered angrily, "Ricky, WHAT ARE YOU DOING???"

"The whole family came!" he whispered back to her. "Plus, I let you down the other day, sis, but I'm here now to make you look good. Trust me!" Then he began to rap.

"Yo, Jordan Jamz and Darren Dill
Took shots at my sister
That were kinda ill.
I let her down,
But not today,
I'mma kick it old style
On the auditorium stage!"

He started to pop and lock, then dropped to the floor and spun around the stage.

Maria put her head in her hands. *This can't be happening*, she thought.

Ricky bumped into one of Megs's teammates, then accidentally got in the way of a froosbetball Megs had just tossed to another teammate. The froosbetball hit him hard in the back.

"OW! Hey, Megs! You did that on purpose!" said Ricky.

"I did not!" said Megs.

"You sure did! Give me that . . . that . . . *whatever-you-call-it-ball*!" Ricky said as he made a grab for the disk.

"You're ruining the tryouts!" Megs growled.

"I'm trying to help!" Ricky growled right back.

"Stop it, you two!" Maria yelled. "YOU'RE WRECKING EVERYTHING!"

Stunned by his sister's anger, Ricky let go just as Megs tugged on the ball with all her might. She lost her grip, and the froosbetball flew offstage. It sailed right at their father, who was waiting in the wings, and hit him in the noggin.

Sal was worried that The Great Bathroom Incident No One Should Ever Bring Up Again may have affected his daughter's chances to become mascot. So he planned to surprise the audience with free bowls of his nearly-award-winning chili! Everyone would be so happy, they would definitely vote for Maria.

He wanted to be ready to ladle it out as soon as Maria was done, so when she went onstage he'd snuck behind the curtain, holding a giant vat of chili in his arms.

But then the fought-over froosbetball came flying at his head at a million miles an hour. The ball knocked him senseless, and the vat of chili fell, spilling gallons of the slippery, greasy stuff all over the stage floor.

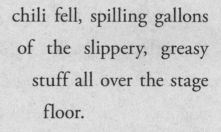

Maria, Ricky, Megs, and the whole froosbetball team found themselves slipping, sliding, and then falling in the huge slick of chili that flowed across the stage. Maria staggered to her feet and then immediately fell again, covering herself in beans and tomatoes.

Then, as if things couldn't possibly get any worse, her little two-year-old sister, Scoochy, suddenly appeared out of nowhere, sliding across the stage on her belly like she was at a water park . . . Naturally, she had taken off all her clothes.

"WHEEEEEE!" she shouted, sliding past Maria, her tiny toddler butt visible to all.

That sight was simply too much for the audience. Everyone began to laugh.

And not just in the school. All over San Pimento, people watching the competition on live television broke into fits of laughter. They giggled and snorted and chortled and guffawed. Some even laughed so hard that they peed a little. If they happened to be drinking milk, it poured through their noses.

It was Maria's worst nightmare. Except this was really happening. Her family had embarrassed her more than anyone had ever been embarrassed in the history of the universe. Her face red with humiliation and tomatoes, she finally made it to her feet and shouted into the microphone:

"THAT'S IT! I QUIT!!!"

The students in the auditorium went quiet. Ms. Macaroon walked delicately out to the stage. "You mean, you quit the competition?"

Maria turned to her, fury blazing in her eyes.

"No. *I quit the Peppers.*"

CHAPTER 8

"But . . . but . . . you can't just *quit* a family!" cried her mother, Tee.

Sal agreed. "It's our family motto: Peppers grow in bunches, and bunches means together!"

Ms. Macaroon had gathered the entire Pepper family in her office. Maria sat with crossed arms. Her brothers and sisters stood behind her in silence. Sal was still slightly dizzy from the froosbetball. The nurse had given him some ice for his head.

"Actually, I'm afraid she can. It's been done before," said Ms. Macaroon.

"When? How? Who?" the Pepper family asked at the same time.

"*I* did it. Two years ago. With my own family." Darren Dill IV had just walked into Ms.

Macaroon's office along with his butler, Crinklebottom.

The Peppers all stared at him.

"A couple of years ago, I had my family declared *embarrassum totalus*. Translated from the Latin: *totally embarrassing*. It's a legal tool that I used to leave them once and for all."

"But I thought you were an orphan," Maria said suspiciously.

"I *am* an orphan. By choice. My parents live in Girder City."

"But why?" Sal cried. "What did they ever do to you?"

Darren shook his head. "They wanted me to have fun, goof around, and get involved in the *disgusting* family business. But their antics embarrassed me. I prefer order and perfection in all things. They didn't understand me at all.

So I divorced them. And Crinklebottom helped me do it!"

The butler bowed shakily.

CRINKLE

"In addition to being a master deejay, Crinklebottom is also a very talented lawyer. He'll take Maria's case and use the same argument he used against my family: that you, the Peppers, are so *totally*, completely embarrassing that you are ruining your daughter's life! All

Maria needs is a place to live and a guardian to look after her. Crinklebottom and I will be her new family."

Her brothers and sisters piped up.

"Maria may be a total perfectionist . . ." said Annie.

"And kinda bossy . . ." agreed Beta.

"And super fussy . . ." Ricky concurred.

"But she'd never leave us!" cried Megs. "A Pepper quitting the Peppers! HAW! That's ridiculous!"

Maria's eyes became angry slits.

She nodded. "That is EXACTLY what I want. I'm so, so *sick* of you guys! I work so hard to make everything perfectly perfect, but every time I think I finally have my life in order, you all come along and ruin it for me! You destroy my school projects, interrupt my plays, embarrass me in front of my friends, and now *the whole city* is laughing at me because of you! I DON'T WANT TO BE A PEPPER ANYMORE!"

Every jaw in the family dropped.

But before they could say a single thing, Maria, Darren, and Crinklebottom marched out of Ms. Macaroon's office.

Annie saw Darren smile as he closed the door.

Maria was in total awe of Darren's apartment.

It wasn't just that the penthouse was super fancy, which it most definitely was.

It was that Darren's entire apartment was perfectly, *perfectly* perfect.

Inside, everything was white and crystal and stunning. The gigantic windows were spotless and glinted in the sunlight. Shoes were taken off at the door and put away in a special drawer that came out from the wall automatically, then slid away again, hiding any stinky smells.

Crinklebottom immediately snapped on a pair of white gloves the minute they entered the apartment, and started dusting right away.

White leather furniture didn't have any crayon marks or chewed-up ends from wild two-year-olds. No lacrosse sticks, half-eaten

bags of chips, or horror movie magazines littered the floor and the end tables.

Maria poked her head in the kitchen. The counters weren't covered with chili ingredients. Appliances gleamed and sparkled as though they had never been touched. But this wasn't the case at all, because there was a sweet smell of blueberry pie baking in the oven. And here she wouldn't have to fight with five brothers and sisters for a slice of it.

"Would you like to see your room?" Darren asked with a smile.

He led Maria down the hallway.

Maria glanced briefly at the door marked TOP SECRET.

Darren saw her looking. "You can enter any room in this apartment, except that one . . . Right this way."

Down a hallway they came to a door that had Maria's name on it. Darren opened the door to the largest (and cleanest) bedroom Maria had ever seen!

There was another door that led to a private bathroom and walk-in closet already full of clothes.

"Crinklebottom did some shopping for you. You wouldn't think it, but the old guy has pretty good taste," he said.

"No more messes." Maria smiled. And the best part? Annie's stuff was nowhere in sight.

She walked over to a bed so precisely made that she wasn't even sure she had the courage to climb into it and mess it up. A copy of *How to Make Friends, Influence People, and Crush Your Enemies into Dust* lay on the bedside table.

Darren Dill smiled. "A messy bed means a messy life."

That night, Crinklebottom prepared them an amazing meal. No one spilled any drinks on her plate. No toddlers threw food in her hair.

After dinner, Maria thought it might be fun to play a game.

"How about crazy eights or Monopoly? Crinklebottom, you could play, too."

"Kids' games," Darren laughed. "Too many pieces that could get lost under coffee tables and couches. I've been having fun memorizing the dictionary! I'm all the way up to *K*!"

Over the next few weeks, Maria began to notice that living with Darren and Crinklebottom was very different from life with her own family.

First, it was really quiet. Ricky wasn't practicing his break-dancing in the living room, and Scoochy wasn't running around naked and screaming at the top of her lungs. And even though Maria had dreamed of a house free from their noise, sometimes it was so quiet in Darren's apartment that she couldn't concentrate.

Once in a while Darren would play the violin or some classical music, but never anything you could dance to. Maria used to love it when Annie would start a dance party in the den.

Nothing was ever shattered by soccer balls, basketballs, or even froosbetballs. (In fact, no balls were allowed.) Maria had always made a habit of picking up whichever ball was lying around and fiddling with it while she worked on her homework. She was surprised to find she kind of missed it.

And while Crinklebottom cooked amazing meals, they were always fancy things like duck liver and octopus salad. Once, Maria asked if they could have burgers or macaroni and cheese for a change. Or maybe even chili! Crinklebottom raised an eyebrow and Darren snorted. "Ha ha!" laughed Darren. "That's a good one, Maria!"

Whenever she asked how his San Pimento Olive training was going, Darren curiously changed the subject.

He was perfectly polite, of course.

"There's a time and place for everything," he told her. "And we do not discuss mascots at the dinner table."

Maria sighed. She'd wanted to live an orderly life, but rules for dinner conversation may have been taking it a little far.

At school, Maria ignored her brothers and sisters. She didn't wave when she saw Annie in

the hallway. She didn't watch the froosbetball team practice their moves. She didn't smile when Beta filmed Ms. Macaroon's chocolate milk mustache.

And though Maria thought about getting in the lunch line, she was a little afraid to see her father's sad face. Besides, she and Darren sat at their own special lunch table. Darren said it was important for her not to talk to her family until the divorce was final.

CHAPTER 9

Meanwhile, a dark cloud hung over the Pepper house.

Ricky stopped break-dancing. Megs no longer played sports. Scoochy dressed their pet pig, Oink, in a dress and wig and started calling him by Maria's name. "SCOOCHY SORRY, MARIA. COME HOME!" Tee went to bed

with Maria's picture every night. Sal even lost interest in cooking chili.

The only two family members with any energy at all were Annie and Beta.

They sat on the school steps one afternoon, watching Maria and Darren drive off in the limousine.

Beta cleaned his camera while Annie tapped her chin with her microphone.

"Darren and Crinklebottom are keeping a secret. There's something real fishy about them," she noted.

"Well, sure," Beta agreed. "That's because they stink!"

Annie shook her head. "No, I mean there's something weird about those two. Someone should figure out what they're up to."

Beta looked up, a glint in his eye. "You mean . . . someone should *investigate* them?"

Annie nodded. "That's EXACTLY what I mean."

They decided the best place to research Darren Dill IV was the library.

They wanted to find out exactly why Darren had divorced his own family. There had to be a story on it somewhere. A kid divorcing his own family had to be big news, even in Girder City!

After hours of reading old news articles, Annie hit pay dirt. She called Beta over to read with her.

BOY LEAVES FAMOUS MASCOT FAMILY!

Seven-year-old Darren Dill IV is divorcing his family, a dynasty of professional sports mascots dating back to the court of King Louis XIV.

The Dills were attending Darren's violin recital when the boy flew into a rage. Multiple witnesses recall the family parading around in large plush outfits, starting the wave, and cartwheeling up and down the aisles.

Said Darren, "I'm not some cheering animal. But they don't understand what's important to me. So I want a divorce!"

Since then, the Dills have decided to hang up their giant stuffed animal heads.

"After Darren left, none of us seemed to have any pep left," says Darren Dill III.

Darren's mother, Diana, agrees. "Darren took our costumes when he left. But that's okay. Air horns make me cry now, anyway."

"I just want our son to know we're sorry," adds Darren Dill III. "We should have accepted him as he is."

The Dill Family, in happier times...

Annie and Beta read the article in silence. Then they looked at each other. "We need to call a family meeting," they said together.

Later that night, the Peppers gathered around the dining room table.

Annie and Beta passed around the article they had found.

"Air horns and flips during a violin recital? Ouch!" Megs said.

Annie nodded. "It's awful. But that's not why I called this meeting."

"Then why did you make us read such a sad story?" cried Sal. "We already knew Darren divorced his family!"

"Don't you see?" said Annie. "There's only one thing that Darren hates more than his family . . ."

Tee snapped her fingers. "Mascots!"

"That's right!" Megs said. "He called the family business 'disgusting' in Ms. Macaroon's office, remember?"

Beta nodded. "And remember during the television interview when he said his parents would be shocked about his competing for school mascot? Boy, would they!"

"If he hates mascots so much, then why would he try so hard to become the Pimento Olive?" asked Ricky.

Annie shook her head. "That's what I'd like to know. And I bet Maria would, too."

Sal stood up. "Remember the Pepper family rule: If you poke the Peppers . . . Peppers positively poke back!"

The Peppers all nodded.

Meemaw Pepper dug around in her handbag and pulled out a ninja mask. "Let's go get our girl," she said as she pulled the mask down over her face.

CHAPTER 10

Of course, it wasn't quite as simple as that. Darren had stationed huge security guards in the lobby to make sure no unwanted guests got in—especially guests like the Peppers. His lobby guards looked mean, muscly, and not the least bit friendly.

Annie went in first, pretending to be a friend of Maria's who was there to get a homework assignment she had missed.

"If you don't live on the premises, Mr. Dill says you gotta scram!" said one guard.

"But I need to get that homework!"

Another guard shook his head. "No one gets in without Mr. Dill giving the say-so. Now make like a tree and leave!"

The Peppers crouched behind the food truck and discussed their next move.

"We'll have to sneak in, but we need a distraction," hissed Tee.

Sal smiled. "I have an idea!"

Darren's armed security force watched the Chili Chikka-Wow-Wow drive up to the entrance. A big, round man with a funny mustache got out and came running up to them. They got out their batons.

"Hey! Can you guys tell me . . . is this 20 Second Street?"

"Naw, dude. 20 Second Street is all the way across town. This is 22nd Street!"

Sal looked at the slip of paper in his hand and sighed. "Nuts. My chili won't be piping hot if I have to drive it all the way across town!"

One of the guards looked interested. "Hey, did you say chili?"

Another guard rubbed his stomach. "Mmm. Man, I'm *starving*. Chili sure sounds good!"

The other two guards nodded, licking their lips at the thought.

"Well, you guys have been super helpful . . ." Sal snapped his fingers. "Hey, how about a cup for each of you? On the house!" He ran to the truck, then came back with three cups of chili.

Soon the big guards were chowing down. Between spoonfuls, one of them burped loudly and said, "Wow! This is some great chili! What kind did you say it was?"

A big grin stretched across Sal's face. "I call it Sal's Seriously Spicy Sriracha Chili."

Five minutes later the floor was empty of guards. The bathrooms, however, were full.

Sal waved the rest of the family inside. "They'll be in the bathroom for an hour, at least. Let's go!"

"Wait a minute!" cried Beta. He ran over to the computer bank and tapped a few buttons.

"Hmm," he said. "There's more security on Darren's floor. He has laser beam alarms and cameras. We'll have to get through all of that to get into the apartment."

Tee reminded them of another family rule: "Peppers press on!"

They took the elevator to the top floor. When the doors opened, they saw that Beta was right.

"Darren's not taking any chances. He has twenty-four-hour cameras pointed everywhere," he confirmed. "And of course getting through the lasers won't be easy. If you so much as brush one, it will alert the police!"

Megs nodded. "Leave the cameras to me."

She pulled out her froosbetball. She dribbled a couple of times, took aim, then threw the inflated disk like a Frisbee.

It zinged down the hallway and bounced off one camera, breaking it. Then it rebounded to the next camera, breaking that, then the third, and the fourth, and finally returned to her waiting hand.

Megs spun the froosbetball victoriously on her finger. "The game of the future!" she said with a big smile.

"Great work, Megs, but we still have the

lasers to worry about. The button to turn them off is at the other end of the hallway," said Beta sadly.

"Leave those to me," Ricky piped up.

He put on his headphones. Then he cracked his knuckles, shook himself loose, and began to break-dance past the first beams.

He was hypnotic to watch!

Ricky did the worm past six or seven of them. He popped and locked past the next four.

He dropped, kicked, leapt, and spun on his head past even more.

And when he finally reached the end of the hall, he did some robot moves and pushed the button. Instantly the laser beams vanished.

Darren's apartment was quiet. And dark. And tastefully decorated.

The Peppers tiptoed around, not sure where to look.

"Whew!" Sal whispered. "This place is fancy with a capital *F*!"

"All this white carpeting!" Tee shook her head. "Should we take off our shoes?"

Annie hissed, "Peppers! Focus!"

They crept down the hallway, peeking through doorways and poking in drawers.

As Tee looked around, she noticed something was amiss. "Scoochy? Sal! I think we lost Scoochy!"

He shrugged. "You know her . . . probably just breaking something expensive."

Annie led them to the door marked TOP SECRET that she had seen in the television interview. "If Darren's up to something, my guess is we'll find it in this room!"

Carefully they opened the door and walked inside.

Right away, a siren started blaring loudly.

Then a huge net, which the Peppers hadn't noticed was laid out on the floor, scooped them up and left them dangling like a bunch of grapes in the air.

"Fiddle-faddle!" grumbled Meemaw Pepper through her ninja mask.

CHAPTER 11

Moments later, the family was surrounded by Darren, Crinklebottom, and Maria. Sal waved sheepishly.

It was Maria's first time in the TOP SECRET room, and she tried to make sense of what she was seeing.

The long room was filled with animal head trophies, all mounted to the wall. But they weren't *actually* animal heads. These were mounted mascot costume heads. There had to be at least fifty of them!

A large shredding machine sat in the center of the room. And in front of it lay the San Pimento Olive mascot costume. But none of this confused Maria as much as the sight of her family dangling from the ceiling.

"Mom? Dad? What are you doing here?" Maria cried.

"How delightful!" Darren clapped happily. "A family reunion!"

"We came to rescue you, pumpkin!" said Sal. "That Darren's up to no good!"

"What are you talking about?" asked Maria.

Annie growled. "Why don't you tell her,

Darren? You never wanted to be the Pimento Olive! You hate mascots!"

Annie tossed the newspaper article down to her sister.

Maria caught it and read quickly. Then she looked up at Darren. "I don't understand. You *hate* mascots?"

Darren laughed. "I don't hate mascots. I *loathe* them." He ran his fingers along the fake purple fur of the Parsippany Panther. "I come from a family of mascots, dating back hundreds of years. Except I *detest* mascots. I wanted to play the violin in an orchestra. But my family laughed at me. My father paid for *air horn* lessons instead."

Slowly Darren began to pull the panther's whiskers out one by one. "I wouldn't give up my dream. I practiced in secret for months for my first violin recital. But my family found out and ruined everything. So, I divorced them. And I made sure my part of the family fortune included their precious costumes!"

Maria was confused. "I don't understand. If you hate mascots so much, why would you work so hard to become the San Pimento Olive?"

"I thought shredding the family costumes and hanging their heads on the wall as trophies would be the perfect revenge. But it wasn't perfect enough. I want to destroy every mascot in the world! So I came up with the perfect plan. Crinklebottom and I move around to different schools. I win their mascot competitions, shred the costumes, and then move on with a new trophy for my wall."

Darren turned to Maria. "But I've had that

Olive costume for weeks, and just haven't had the heart to shred it . . . because of you. You've had to put up with the same stuff I have. A family who ruins everything for you! But now that my secret is out, Crinklebottom and I will have to leave tonight. Come with us, Maria." He held his hand out to her.

Maria looked up at her family. Sal was licking chili from his mustache while Annie and Beta squabbled over the lighting in the cell phone video they were filming. Tee tried to stop Megs from spinning her froosbetball. Meemaw smacked her hearing aid loudly. And Ricky's robot dance moves made the whole net shake.

Maria couldn't believe it, but she had missed them.

They hadn't tried to mess up her dreams like Darren's family had. Not really. Ricky had only jumped onstage because he had let her down at the rap battle. And Annie and Beta had asked to interview Maria first, but she said no. Megs even let Maria take credit for a whole new sport!

In that moment, Maria realized something.

She *loved* her silly family.

"No, Darren. I can't go with you." Maria looked up at her family. "Sometimes you guys totally mess up my plans, but I know now that it's only because you love me. And I guess I'm not so perfect, either," she added. "I want to come home."

Sal wiped away a tear. "That's just wonderful, pumpkin," he said. "But first, could you cut us down?"

Maria moved to set them free, but then a pair of shaky hands grabbed her.

It was Crinklebottom. Maria tried to wriggle free, but for an old guy he was surprisingly strong!

Darren shook his head. "Too bad. We would have been a perfect family, Maria. I guess I'll have that Olive head on my wall after all."

He walked over to the shredder and flipped a switch. It turned on with a loud roar. Sharp metal teeth looked hungry for the plush mascot costume.

Darren lifted up the Olive costume and moved to feed it into the machine.

Maria screamed, "NO! STOP!"

But Darren was relishing this moment. He held the Olive costume closer and closer to the

grinding metal teeth. Soon it was less than an inch from being ground up.

Then, deep in the shadows of the room, something moved.

Darren stopped and squinted as the oddly familiar shadow lurched into the light.

It was a unicorn head . . . his father's!

The head moved jerkily toward them.

"I destroyed you!" Darren yelled. "YOU CAN'T BE REAL!!!"

The unicorn head only came closer.

Crinklebottom may have been a good butler, an amazing deejay, and a really good lawyer, but he wasn't at all brave. With a high-pitched shriek, he let go of Maria and ran from the room.

"Get back!" Darren screamed as the unicorn head inched toward him. Then he fell to the floor and covered his head with his hands, scared that the mascot costume had come back for revenge.

But then, something unexpected happened. The unicorn head *giggled*. It was the sort of giggle a toddler might make.

Wait a minute . . . thought Maria.

Maria rolled her eyes and lifted the unicorn head, revealing Scoochy underneath.

The two-year-old grinned. "PEEKABOO, MARIA!"

Thankfully, Scoochy still had her clothes on.

CHAPTER 12

Two months later

"Hello! This is Annie Pepper with SPN News, broadcasting live at the San Pimento home-coming parade! It's a beautiful fall day here in San Pimento, and in just a moment, we'll see the first floats go by."

Annie turned to Beta and whispered loudly, "Beta, that's your cue to turn the camera toward the parade!"

"Sorry, sis!" Beta said as he adjusted his lens.

Annie smoothed her hair and smiled. "First up is the talented San Pimento Grade School marching band. Boy, can they jam! Following the band is the limousine of the world-famous Dill mascot family, recently reunited with their son."

The night of the Pepper break-in had been life changing for Darren. He read the article that Annie and Beta had discovered. And when he found out that his parents had given up mascoting because they understood how much they had hurt him, he forgave them for everything. Darren had moved back home and was now happily taking violin lessons. And with

Darren's full support, the Dills had put their furry costumes and plush heads on once again!

"Next up we have the San Pimento junior froosbetball team, led by their captain, Megs Pepper!" Annie announced. "You know, that wacky combination of basketball and Frisbee has really taken San Pimento by storm!"

The rap and break-dancing float rolled by. "And here's the world-famous Jordan Jamz performing his newest hit, with break-dancing backup by none other than Ricky Pepper!"

Beta had uploaded a Y'allTube video of Ricky break-dancing around the laser beams in Darren's apartment, and Ricky had become quite the celebrity.

Annie jumped up and down excitedly. "Ooo! Ooo!" she cried.

"Keep still!" said Beta.

"I can't help it!" Annie replied. "It's the moment we've all been waiting for, folks! Here comes the new San Pimento Olive, Maria Pepper, riding on top of her family's food truck, the Chili Chikka-Wow-Wow. And what a perfect Pimento Olive she is! Look at her, blowing kisses and throwing the traditional homecoming pimento olives to the crowd! I think this may be just about the best San Pimento homecoming celebration we've ever seen. Thanks for joining us! This is Annie Pepper signing off for SPN News, saying, 'Have a great day, San Pimento, and a Pepper tomorrow!'"

From her place on the float, Maria spotted Roger and Lavonia cheering her on. Sal's mustache bounced with joy as he drove his food truck. Behind them, her mother had lifted Scoochy onto her shoulders so she could blow a

sloppy kiss to Darren and the rest of the Dills. Everyone Maria cared about was having a perfectly wonderful time.

It looked like her favorite book really did have the best advice. The final chapter of the book *How to Make Friends, Influence People, and Crush Your Enemies into Dust* said it all:

Vlad the Impaler taught his little brother how to ride a bike. Attila the Hun never missed his grammy's birthday. You may be the most bloodthirsty, vicious warlord in the world, but it's still nice to make time for family.

The End?*

---

* No! The Peppers will be back in *The Pepper Party Is Completely Cursed*!

Can't get enough Pepper pandemonium?
Read on for a sneak peek of this
feisty family's
next crazy catastrophe!

A frightening night of fortune-telling
finds Beta cracking a crystal ball and
reawakening an old family curse. Can the
Peppers prevent a spooky string of strange
sightings from turning their home into
a real house of horrors?

MEET THE PEPPERS.

FUNNY RUNS IN THE FAMILY.

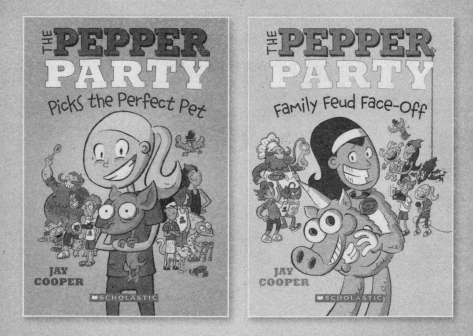

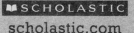